P9-DOB-938

P9-DOB-938

JOAN STEINER

LOOK-ALIKES™ JR.

Photography by Thomas Lindley

Little, Brown and Company
BOSTON   NEW YORK   LONDON

For T.C.

The author wishes to express heartfelt thanks to Thomas Lindley for his superb photographic work, and to Megan Shaw Tingley, her editor, and Amy Berkower, her agent, for the unflagging support and enthusiasm they have shown for Look-Alikes from the very beginning. Thanks also go to Paul Richer of *Sesame Street* magazine, who originally commissioned several of these images.

Copyright © 1999 by Joan Steiner

The Bedroom scene was photographed by Jeff Heiges.

All rights reserved. No part of this book may be reproduced in any form or by any electronic or mechanical means, including information storage and retrieval systems, without permission in writing from the publisher, except by a reviewer who may quote brief passages in a review.

All brand-name products are trademarks of their respective owners.

First Edition

Library of Congress Cataloging-in-Publication Data

Steiner, Joan (Joan Catherine)
    Look-alikes jr. / Joan Steiner ; photography by Thomas Lindley — 1st ed.
      p. cm.
    Summary: Simple verses challenge readers to identify the everyday objects used to construct eleven three-dimensional scenes, including a house, kitchen, bedroom, school bus, train, farm, and rocket.
    ISBN 0-316-81307-9
    1. Picture puzzles — Juvenile literature. [1. Picture puzzles.] I. Lindley, Thomas, ill. II. Title. III. Title: Look-alikes junior.
    GV1507.P47S747   1999
    793.73—DC21   99-11683

10 9 8 7 6 5 4 3 2

LB

Printed in the United States of America

The illustrations in this book are photographs of three-dimensional collages created from found objects. The text was set in Formata. The display type is Hoffman.

C ome visit a land of wild surprises
Where common objects wear disguises!
Peanuts can look like a teddy bear,
Kiwi fruit like the pad for a chair.
At least fifty look-alikes in each scene
 (but two).
Find some or all—it's up to you.
The candy clock will count the hours,
As you test your detective powers...
And if you're really keeping track,
You'll find all listed at the back!

Happy Hunting!

To Look-Alike Land! We're blasting full throttle
On a spaceship that looks like a THERMOS BOTTLE.

Let's start our visit at this house.
That rock on the lawn looks like a TOY MOUSE!

Here's the kitchen, right down the hall.
That tea kettle looks like a red CHRISTMAS BALL.

The parlor's a cozy place to sit
In a chair that looks like an OVEN MITT.

Here's the bedroom and the bathroom as well.
The sink in the bathroom looks like a SHELL.

Here's the school bus, right on time.
Each rearview mirror looks like a DIME.

This classroom has books and paints and blocks.
The teacher's desk looks like a TISSUE BOX.

We hope that you will come back soon!
The signal post looks like a WOODEN SPOON.
It's signaling *"Bye, bye—for now!"*

CHOO-CHOO TRAIN

- *46 Look-Alikes*

SMOKE: Clumps of cotton. TRAIN: **Locomotive:** Sink aerator, jar of model paint, tiny brass bracket, roll of film, lamp socket, yellow Life Saver candy*, flashlight, spiral notepad, toy school bus, pennies, spool of black thread, big black buttons, tiny paper binder clip, can opener, wrench, (artificial) daisies. **Tender:** Tea tin with tea, sewing machine bobbins (on next two cars as well). **Passenger car:** Watercolor paint box, pencils, birthday candles, melba toast, afro comb, package-carrying handle, dog biscuits, dollar bill, corncob holder. **Freight car:** Ruler, batteries, fishing float, tiny key, more pennies, wallet, dollar bills, clothing label. LANDSCAPE: Green blanket, tweed jacket, woolen hat, parsley, jigsaw pieces. SIGNAL POST: Wooden spoon, top of a Thermos, red and green Life Saver candies. TRACKS: Brown lamp cord, sticks of gum (unwrapped).

ANSWER TO EXTRA CHALLENGE: Pencil.

JOAN STEINER is a graduate of Barnard College and the recipient of numerous art and design awards, including a Society of Illustrators Award and a National Endowment for the Arts fellowship. Her first book, *Look-Alikes*, received glowing reviews and was featured on the *Today* show and *CBS This Morning*. Ms. Steiner lives in Claverack, New York.